For Emma Abercrombie Peters
—B. A.

For David Michael
—A. G.

Margaret K. McElderry Books
An imprint of Simon & Schuster Children's Publishing Division
1230 Avenue of the Americas, New York, New York 10020
Text copyright © 2002 by Barbara Abercrombie
Illustrations copyright © 2002 by Adam Gustavson
Book design by Kristin Smith
The text for this book is set in Bembo.
The illustrations are rendered in oils.
Printed in Hong Kong
10 9 8 7 6 5 4 3 2 1

Library of Congress Cataloging-in-Publication Data
Abercrombie, Barbara.
Bad dog, Dodger! / by Barbara Abercrombie ; illustrated by Adam Gustavson.— 1st ed.
p. cm.
Summary: Nine-year-old Sam decides to teach his new puppy to behave, but not before Dodger has scared his sister, pulled down some curtains, and stopped a baseball game.
ISBN 0-689-83782-8
[1. Dogs—Training—Fiction. 2. Pets—Fiction. 3. Animals—Infancy—Fiction.] I. Gustavson, Adam, ill. II. Title.
PZ7.A1614 Bad 2002
[E]—dc21
00-046578

BAD DOG, DODGER!

WRITTEN BY **barbara abercrombie**

ILLUSTRATED BY **adam gustavson**

Margaret K. McElderry Books
New York London Toronto Sydney Singapore

Sam wanted a dog.

"If you're a good boy," said his father.

"When you can take care of it yourself," said his mother.

Sam cleaned up his room.

He ate carrots and broccoli.

He stopped making
monster noises at night
to scare Molly,
his older sister.

He hung up his cap after baseball practice.
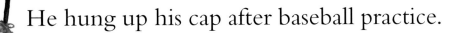

On the morning of his ninth birthday,
Sam found a large box waiting for him.

Inside was a puppy. He was black and soft and had big feet.
Sam named him Dodger.

The whole family loved Dodger. Dodger
licked their faces and curled up on their laps.
He nibbled their shoelaces.

One day Dodger knocked the trash all over
the kitchen floor. "Bad dog, Dodger!" said Sam.

Dodger wagged his tail and wanted to play,
but Sam was already late for baseball practice.

When Molly was taking a bath one night,
Dodger jumped into the tub with her. She started
to scream. Dodger jumped out and raced through
the house dripping water.

Sam and his father chased him with towels.
"Bad dog, Dodger!" yelled Sam.
"He's not bad," said his father. "He just wants
to play."

One morning Sam found Dodger chewing his baseball cap. There was a big hole in it.

Sam was so mad he almost cried.

They were eating dinner when Dodger pulled
down the living room curtains. He wore them into
the kitchen. He looked like a bride.

"I've had it," said Sam's mother. "This dog has to
live outside."

The next day Dodger jumped over the fence and followed Sam to school and into his classroom.

He knocked over the hamster cage. He ate the
cover off a spelling book. Sam's mother had to leave
work to take Dodger home.

Saturday was Sam's first Little League game. He was up at bat when Dodger came flying onto the field.

The umpire yelled, "Time out!"

The other team booed.

The coach yelled, "Get that dog!"

Dodger grabbed the bat and ran around the field
with it. The umpire and the coach ran after him.
Sam had to leave the game to take Dodger home.

"We can't go on like this," said Sam's mother. "Maybe Dodger would be better off with somebody who had more time."

Sam knew his mother was right. Dodger needed more attention.

Sam went out and sat in the doghouse
with Dodger. "I love you, Dodger."
Dodger's tail thumped up and down. "But
you need to practice being a good dog."
Suddenly Sam had an idea.
That night he set his alarm to go off
half an hour early.

The family was still asleep when Sam got up the next morning. In the kitchen he filled his pockets with dog treats.

"Wake up, Dodger!"

Sam pitched a ball to Dodger. Dodger caught it.

"Good dog, Dodger!"

Sam waved a treat in the air.
"Come!"
Dodger pranced around the yard
with the ball in his mouth. "This is
training, not a game!" yelled Sam.

Finally Dodger set the ball down at Sam's feet.
Sam gave him a treat and said, "Good dog, Dodger."

"Dodger's in spring training," Sam told his parents at breakfast.

Sam pitched balls to Dodger every morning. "Come, Dodger!" he'd shout, waving a treat when Dodger caught the ball.

"Sit!" And Sam would push Dodger's bottom down to show him what sit meant. "Stay!"

After a month of training Sam decided Dodger
was ready to come to a baseball game.

Dodger sat in the bleachers next to Sam's parents.

In the ninth inning Sam was up at bat with two strikes and the bases loaded. The score was tied. The pitcher wound up to pitch. Everybody held their breath. Sam gripped the bat and hit a fly ball over the bleachers.

"Foul!" yelled the umpire. Suddenly a flash of black fur leaped into the air to catch the ball.

Oh, no, thought Sam as the umpire called "Time out!" and the game stopped. "That crazy dog again!" cried the coach. The other team was laughing. Sam's mother was shaking her head.

Dodger trotted toward Sam with the ball in his mouth. He dropped it at Sam's feet. "Good dog," said Sam.

He walked Dodger to the dugout. "Sit." Dodger sat.

All the spectators grew very quiet. The other
team stopped laughing.

"Stay," said Sam.
Dodger stayed.

Sam hit the next pitch right over the fence for a home run. He ran to first, second, third base.

As he reached home plate, he called, "Come, Dodger!" and everyone clapped. Even the coach.

After the game the team had their picture taken. Dodger was in the front row and got to wear Sam's baseball cap.